Adrian at
LOGGERHEADS

Adrian at
LOGGERHEADS

MARIO HERBERT

CONTENTS

Introduction

This is the story of Adrian Manning, a fifteen-year-old boy who has been trying his earnest best to attain popularity for over two years.

He travelled on dangerous buses, faced dangerous bullies and found himself in incredibly disastrous situations all in the name of attaining and maintaining popularity.

These disasters were chronicled in *Adrian at Large* and *Adrian at Last*, but Adrian is evolving—he's finally finished with his popularity-focused schemes.

What is Adrian ultimately evolving into?

Does this evolution signal an end to his disastrous adventures, or do the disasters evolve as well to meet the new Adrian?

Answers lie ahead, so turn the page and let the adventures begin!

THE EVOLUTION OF ADRIAN MANNING

Adrian walked across the hardcourt in the middle of the school, in the early morning breeze. He stepped with a perky confidence, en route to his classroom after a period in the science lab. He beamed with pride as he walked past the juniors; just a couple of months ago, he was a third former in short pants, looking up to the senior students. Now, he was the one in long pants and a tie, and he was convinced that these juniors were looking at him with the same admiration he had for his seniors a couple of months ago.

As he climbed a narrow flight of stairs, his classroom slowly coming into visibility, a smile graced his face; three days of this new school term had failed to subdue the novelty of his promotion. He briskly entered his new classroom, surrounded by new and different faces, and took his seat at the second of six desks, in the first of four rows.

"New term, new form, new uniform, new classmates and a new Adrian," he thought to himself, as he sat in a partial daze, recounting misfortunes of the past.

For three years he had been obsessed with popularity. He had used his intellect to devise schemes for popularity, which invariably backfired with disastrous results. Now, in this new term, after one too many disasters, he had put popularity behind him, and was excited to see where his intellect would take him as he found better things to focus on. Adrian was hopeful that this new modus operandi would eliminate the disasters which underscored the previous three years.

A girl entered the class and took a seat next to him, at the first desk in the row—it was Sha'Tanya, a dark, hair-gel-abusing girl of average height, who was slim but quite shapely. She was really supposed to be in fifth form, but due to poor academic performance, she was required to repeat her fourth year, making her one of the new additions to Adrian's daily life. Just a year ago, Adrian had the biggest crush on her, but it had perished in a disastrous accident of a date. She was, however, the only friend he had so far in this new class, and likewise, he was the only person in that year group she knew.

As they waited for the teacher to arrive, Adrian and Sha'Tanya struck up a conversation about another new development.

"Hey," Adrian said to Sha'Tanya, "I think I'm going to try the chicken and chips for lunch today."

"Error," Sha'Tanya replied, "they should call that pigeon and cardboard strips."

"What about the rice with lamb stew?"

"Error! I had that yesterday—rice was like bullets

and that sheep had to be receiving a pension," said Sha'Tanya, "my jaw ain't recovered yet."

"You can't be serious!" gasped Adrian. "I had the beef yesterday, and my fork broke trying to penetrate it.

"Cardboard chips, senior citizen lamb, rigor mortis beef—so far everything on the menu is awful."

"Yeah, pretty much," replied Sha'Tanya, with a sympathetic look, "I don't know why they had to change the canteen management."

"Something has to be done about this new canteen," started Adrian, with a ponderous look on his face, "but I'm not sure what can be …"

Their conversation was cut short as a short, stocky, spectacled teacher entered the class and stood behind the teacher's desk, which was centrally positioned at the top of the off-white room, under a huge whiteboard.

"Greetings and felicitations, I am Mrs. Gibbs-Sealy," started the teacher, with zest and a high-pitched voice. "I am commissioned to perfect your mastery of the gloriously nuanced English language."

Sha'Tanya looked at Adrian with a puzzled expression on her face. Adrian just smiled and whispered to her, "I see this is your first time with Mrs. Gibbs-Sealy."

"I will now evaluate your language and public speaking skills," continued the teacher. "You will each stand, give your name, and tell us something about your home, likes and dislikes."

As the teacher gestured to Sha'Tanya to begin, Adrian held his head down; he knew that Sha'Tanya had a tendency to mispronounce certain words, and braced himself for how the language-obsessed teacher would respond.

"My name is Sha'Tanya Carter," started Sha'Tanya, as she rose from her seat. "I come from a big 'fambily'; a lot of people live in my house."

Mrs. Gibbs-Sealy's eyes widened as Sha'Tanya continued.

"I like a good, action 'flim', and I don't like 'bull-cows'."

"That was atrocious," screamed the teacher in her shrill voice, "'fambily', 'flim', 'bull-cows'—those … are … not … words!"

The children laughed as Mrs. Gibbs-Sealy continued, hitting the desk as she spoke.

"Family, film and cows—those are the words which should have been enunciated."

"What's the difference, Ma'am?" asked Sha'Tanya, quizzically.

"Ignoramus," shouted the teacher, in a rage, "my granddaughter in preschool has better command of language than you do. Reunite your posterior with that chair!"

"Huh?"

"Sit at once!"

The class laughed as Sha'Tanya took her seat, while Adrian kept his head down, feeling sorry for her.

"Sha'Tanya's English annoys me too," he thought to himself, "but she didn't deserve to be treated that way."

"Next student!" cried Mrs. Gibbs-Sealy, still in a

rage.

"My name is Adrian Manning," started Adrian, as he rose, mirroring the anger which was rising within him. "I come from a very small household; it's just been my mother and I for the last ten years."

By then, he could feel his rising anger bubbling to a boil.

"I like chess, football and video games," he continued, "but I don't like what you did to Sha'Tanya and I think you owe her an apology."

"I beg your pardon!" cried the teacher, turning red as the class collectively gasped.

Adrian froze for a moment, and it was as if time froze for him. He was inundated with a dichotomy of emotions as his brain caught up with his heart. The anger was still resident; he felt as though his friend was being bullied. However, as his brain processed the words which had just exited his mouth, fear co-signed the lease, becoming roommates with the anger. With all eyes and ears on him, and his heart pounding, Adrian allowed reason to be the landlord.

"With all due respect, Ma'am," he started, looking past his tenants, "your job as a teacher is to inspire us to greatness, but calling a student an ignoramus in front of the class, and comparing her to a pre-schooler is not inspiring at all—it's crushing."

You could have heard a pin drop as Mrs. Gibbs-Sealy sat in the teacher's chair. There was a disagreement within Adrian, and anger had broken the lease, leaving fear the only occupant. Reason had given him the words to say, but it also gave him the knowledge that precedent was not on his side; he had never seen a student win an argument with a teacher.

"I'm not too big to confess that I was in error," said the teacher. "I apologise for any hurt I may have caused you to endure, Sha'Tanya, and I apologise to the class for being less than inspiring."

The class gave Mrs. Gibbs-Sealy a standing ovation, bringing her to tears as Adrian's last remaining tenant was evicted.

Things eventually settled down and the class continued uneventfully. At the end of the period, the bell rang, signalling recess. Mrs. Gibbs-Sealy left the class and the children prepared themselves to do the same. When Adrian rose from his seat, Sha'Tanya hugged him tightly, as the other students gathered around them.

"Thanks for standing up for me," she said, "it means a lot; I won't forget what you did today."

"It was a worthy cause," Adrian replied, "and it actually felt good—once I got past the fear of ..."

"That was really something," interrupted one of their classmates, "no student ever got a teacher to apologise."

"You really know how to put across a point," said another.

"If we could think and talk like you," started Sha'Tanya, putting her arm around Adrian's shoulder, "we could fix a lot of problems in this school."

"Really?" asked Adrian, with scepticism in his voice.

"Like teachers that need to retire," cried one boy.

"Like equipment that's been broken for ages," cried

another.

"Like the food in the canteen!" shouted Sha'Tanya, excitedly as she made eye contact with Adrian.

There was a roar of support for Sha'Tanya's point from the other students—there were different issues affecting the students but everyone was unanimous in the opinion that the new food from the canteen was unacceptable.

"Come on, Adrian, you said something has to be done about the canteen, and you said it feels good standing up for a worthy cause," cried Sha'Tanya. "None of us could ever put forward a case as brilliantly as you would do it."

The class erupted in a chant, "Adrian, Adrian, Adrian!"

Adrian pondered intently. He had been ridiculed for being smart, and he had been praised for being stupid, but he never fathomed that his peers could respect him for his intellect. He had used that intellect to devise schemes for his own elevation; now he had a chance to use it for the elevation of others. He had purposed within himself that he would become a new Adrian in this new school term, and this new dynamic appealed to him—Advocate Adrian was born.

"Alright," said Adrian, "I'll do it!"

The children cheered and exited the classroom with Adrian.

"Go to the principal," Sha'Tanya said to Adrian as they descended the stairs, "I can handle your lunch."

"You sure you can afford that?" asked Adrian, showing his concern openly.

"Error! I can handle getting your lunch, not paying for it," Sha'Tanya replied, with wide eyes and her hands on her hips, "choose your torture."

"I'll take my chances with bullet rice and senior citizen lamb," said Adrian, throwing his hands in the air as if in total despair. "Fingers crossed; this could be the last week we have to put up with this injustice."

Five minutes later, Adrian was standing in the principal's office, facing the principal himself—a tall, slender, clear man, with a pronounced Adam's apple and a hairline in greater withdrawal than an addict in rehab. As he stared at Adrian from behind his large desk, Adrian felt his knees starting to shake a little. Challenging Mrs. Gibbs-Sealy in the classroom, with all the children behind him, was a very different experience. The ambience of the isolated, artificially lit office, and the cold stare of the principal flooded the test tube that was his stomach, with concentrated anxiety.

"You obviously have something to say, young man," said the principal, "let's hear it."

"I'm here to raise a number of concerns on behalf of the student body," said Adrian, diluting the anxiety with a little reason.

"Interesting," said the principal, with a quizzical expression, "let's hear it."

"The students believe that Mr. Peters should be retired."

"Really now?" replied the principal with a straight face.

"I know it might seem like we are overreaching," started Adrian, "but Mr. Peters has been sleeping in classes for years now and it's been affecting our grades."

"Next point!"

"There's a kiln at the back of the school but it's been broken for all the time I've been at the school, disadvantaging the pottery students."

"Kilns are very expensive to fix. We were the last school to operate one."

"Seems to me," started Adrian, with a grin, "the investment would be quite worthwhile; if we were the only school to have a working kiln, we could charge all the other schools a fee to get their pottery baked—it would pay for itself."

"You've got my attention," said Mr. Harding as he grabbed his chin, "what's next?"

Adrian felt triumphant; the students had put a lot of faith in his intellect, and in that moment, his own faith was added to the test tube of his stomach, further diluting the original potion of anxiety.

"The last point I would like to raise is the new canteen management," said Adrian, confidently.

"What about it?" asked the principal, making direct eye contact with Adrian.

"The food is abominable, and speaking on behalf of the student body, we would like to have the old management brought back."

"What makes you think it is appropriate for a principal to discuss management issues with a student?"

"With all due respect, sir," said Adrian, bolstered by the triumph he seemed to gain a moment ago, "the management of the canteen directly impacts the student body, daily. If our nutritional needs are not met, it impacts our ability to learn. I don't think it's out of line to ask that such concerns be heard, and addressed if possible."

There was a hush in the office, as the principal sat, staring intently at Adrian for a moment. He couldn't tell if he had gotten through to Mr. Harding, or if it was the end of the line for Advocate Adrian.

Five minutes later, Adrian approached a predetermined rendezvous point to discover not only his classmates, but some other students from across his year group. Word had spread quickly that he was fighting to get the canteen management changed, along with other issues, and a throng of students were prompting him for good news.

"Well," started Adrian, "he's going to carry out a full investigation of Mr. Peters' performance in class, and he's going to think about fixing the kiln."

"What about the canteen?" shouted Sha'Tanya, to a chorus of solidarity.

"Sorry, guys," started Adrian, with a bewildered look, "there's nothing he can do; the school is legally bound to the new contract for a year."

The students responded with a chorus of sighs and lamentations.

"I don't think I can live with this food for a year," said Sha'Tanya, as she handed Adrian his lunch, "but at least you tried."

Adrian felt bad about his failure; all these people's hopes were raised because they had faith in Advocate Adrian, and he couldn't deliver. He had bought into the idea of using his intellect to fight worthy causes; to fail at this new goal would invalidate this new Adrian.

"This can't be the end of it," Adrian thought to himself, as he looked at the bullet rice lunch container in his hand, "I'm the new Adrian—the Adrian that fights a cause and succeeds; I'm smart enough to figure this out."

"Wait a minute, guys!" cried Adrian, with a gleam in his eyes, as the crowd started to disperse. "We're not finished yet; I think I have a plan."

The next day, when the bell rang for lunch, Adrian and his classmates exited the classroom as usual, but they did not go to the canteen. The dread that had defined lunch time from the start of the term was now replaced with excitement and enthusiasm, as they made their way to the playing field on the southern side of the school.

"Come on," said Adrian, signalling the children to come to the wall on the western side of the field, behind the spectator stands, "the guy's here."

The children rushed to the wall to find a man on a motorcycle on the other side of the wall. Strapped to the back of the cycle was a cooler with forty slices of pizza inside. That section of the wall was lower than most of the other sections, allowing the children to conduct business easily.

"Percy's Pizza was more than happy to accommodate us," Adrian explained, as the children helped themselves to the pizza, "let's make sure they sell out."

The transactions were swiftly occurring until someone noticed one of the school's security guards coming.

"The guard's coming!" cried one of the children, causing the crowd to scatter.

"The bike will meet you at the east of the school," yelled Adrian, as they ran, "the short wall next to the library."

The children who hadn't yet secured pizza, ran to the rendezvous point and the transactions continued until another guard discovered their new location. By that time, everyone had been served and the bike sped away.

A few minutes later, Adrian, Sha'Tanya and some other children were on a bench on the outskirts of the school, consuming their newly sourced lunch.

"This is heaven," said Sha'Tayna, "the flavour … exploding in my mouth like a 'bum'."

"Like a what?" whispered one of the students on the bench.

"She means a bomb," replied Adrian, softly.

At that moment, a boy came marching up to Adrian. He was an average height, medium built, dark Rastafarian with very thick lips. This was Akanni—he was not only a longstanding classmate of Adrian's, but had also been an adversary to him on occasion.

"I never really liked you," started Akanni, "but I gotta hand it to you—this was a brilliant plan, and you even had a 'Plan B'."

Akanni shook Adrian's hand as another student approached. This time it was Alex, a short, dark, chubby boy with fat cheeks and a flat nose. He was a former classmate and long-time friend of Adrian's.

"Congratulations," he said, "you actually spearheaded something that doesn't benefit you alone—that's real growth."

"All these years I wasted my intellect on schemes to become popular, trying to be someone else," said Adrian with a smile, "but I think I've found my calling—I think I've found myself."

"Good for you. Let's just hope this doesn't turn out like past plans you've had."

"Don't jinx it, Alex. Perish the thought," said Adrian, clasping his hands as if in prayer, recounting all the brilliant schemes of the past three years that had all backfired tragically, "failure perished with the old Adrian."

That was the official moment Resistance Adrian was born, and Adrian had high hopes for this new incarnation. The guards were like an occupying force in the school, restricting the masses from accessing decent food, but a new freedom fighter had stepped on the scene.

The next day, at lunch time, the children ran to the south wall again, to get their fill of Percy's Pizza. Unfortunately, the guard was already patrolling that location.

"It was too good to last," cried Alex, as the children gathered several metres from the wall.

"We're not finished yet," said Adrian, "I'm accustomed to setbacks—I plan for them now."

A short while after that, the children were running to another section of the wall. As the guard dashed behind them, Adrian quickly made his way to the original point on the south wall.

"Thirty slices," he shouted over the wall, "and make it quick."

He surrendered the money and was about to receive the slices when the sound of a siren interrupted the transaction. Adrian looked around in the direction of the sound to see a police car approaching. By the time he looked back to the bike, the pizza salesman had mounted it and was speeding off to escape the police.

In a couple of minutes, the children were returning to Adrian for their lunch at the same bench he had eaten on the previous day.

"Where's the food?" asked Alex, on behalf of the group.

"Well, here's the thing," started Adrian, with his heart pounding like a punching bag under attack, "the principal seems to have called in the police."

"So, I gather you didn't get it," said Alex, resulting in a chorus of sighs, "fine, give us back our money so we can hit the canteen."

"Well, here's the thing," started Adrian, again, "I paid for the food just before the police ran the guy off."

"So, wait a minute," started Akanni, with aggressive body language, "you telling me we ain't got money nor food?"

"Pretty much," said Adrian, as fear and anxiety gripped him like an adjustable wrench.

"Error!" shouted Sha'Tanya, as Akanni gripped Adrian by the front of his shirt and forced him against the dingy wall behind the bench.

By that time, all of the children were openly furious, and several of them threatened to furnish Adrian's body with blows. As his heart pounded in his chest, he was sure harm would come to his person, either by way of the students, or the ever-tightening grip of fear and anxiety.

"Calm down," cried Adrian, as reason instinctively asserted itself, "I can fix this!"

"How?" cried Akanni, still holding Adrian up against the wall. "How could you possibly fix this?"

"Distract the guard long enough for me to jump the wall," said Adrian, quickly, "I will go to Percy's Pizza and bring back the food."

"Error," said Sha'Tanya, "that's two districts away."

"That's madness," cried Alex, "Principal Harding would suspend you into oblivion—if he doesn't tear your behind in two."

Akanni released Adrian and looked him in the eyes.

"We need food," he said, "if you think you can get it, I ain't wasting another minute—come."

In a couple of minutes, Akanni was approaching the guard as Adrian approached the wall in the not too far distance.

"Sir," cried Akanni, "on a serious note, what's the issue with the children buying decent food over the wall?"

"If that food poisons you," started the big, tall, clear-skinned guard, "the school's gotta answer to your parents."

Mere metres away, behind the guard's back, Adrian

was climbing the wall. He quickly propelled himself over the top of the wall and landed in the road below. As he picked himself up from the crouched position in which he landed, he was startled by the sound of someone else landing beside him. He turned promptly to see who had followed him over the wall, heart pounding again. To his surprise, it was Sha'Tanya.

"I thought you said this was an 'error'," said Adrian, folding his arms as he stared her in the face.

"It is, but you had my back two days ago when that English teacher had it in for me," replied Sha'Tanya, "so I got your back now."

"Wow. That means a lot."

"Don't get all sappy 'bout it," she replied, with attitude. "Come, I know some 'back roads'."

In that moment, Agent Adrian was born out of necessity, dashing off into foreign territory to retrieve precious artifacts for his homeland. Sha'Tanya led him through some alleys and tracks, moving swiftly, but carefully, to avoid being spotted by police. They reached Percy's Pizza within twenty minutes and completed the transaction.

"If you had gone the main road," said Sha'Tanya, as they started their journey back to the school, "you would still be ten minutes away."

"Thanks for the help," said Adrian, "one of these days, you have to tell me how you know so many shortcuts."

About ten minutes later, Adrian stopped Sha'Tanya in a narrow track, between a fence and some bushes.

"At this rate, we're not going to make it back in

time," he said, "don't you have any more shortcuts up your sleeve."

"Yeah …," said Sha'Tanya, with a pause, "when we come out of this track, you could make the right turn instead of the left—but that would take you through 'The Dead Sea'."

"How much time would it save?"

"About five minutes—but that's 'The Dead Sea'."

"I don't have a choice."

"Error! They don't call it 'The Dead Sea' for nothing; that's one of the most dangerous areas in the country."

"I gotta face my own 'Dead Sea' if I don't get this food to the children before lunch ends," replied Adrian, thinking not only about what Akanni would do to him if he failed, but what failure would say about his latest incarnation, Agent Adrian.

"You said your mother raised you alone for the last ten years," said Sha'Tanya, "I doubt you have what it takes to survive 'The Dead Sea'—but you gotta know."

"You don't know my mother," cried Adrian, "if I can survive her, I can survive anything!"

When they reached the end of the track, Sha'Tanya took her slice of pizza from Adrian and gave him directions.

"Nice knowing you," she said as she went her way, "the canteen's food is bad enough, I ain't trying to eat 'horspital' food too."

Adrian cringed at her mispronunciation of the word 'hospital' but was unmoved by her warning; he had gotten himself through dangerous situations in the past and in that moment, he believed that Agent Adrian was up to the task.

A few minutes later, he was walking through a rundown residential area. As he walked swiftly, he was very conscious of his surroundings. The road upon which he walked was in a state of gross disrepair and the houses were no better. Adrian was surrounded by wooden structures, all of which appeared to have been last painted in the nineteenth century. Between the cracked, weathered paint, Adrian could see holes in the wood, and the windows were no better. Several houses had boarded up windows, where sheets of plywood replaced panes of glass. The very ambience of the area filled Adrian with a sense of despair.

"I can see why they call this place the 'Dead Sea'," Adrian thought to himself.

Just then, a strong smell attacked his nostrils. His heart skipped a beat when he noticed a group of young men on the step of a dilapidated house, smoking. None of them were wearing shirts, and all of them had their pants below the waist, exposing much of their underwear. As Adrian approached them, his heart started pounding like a bass drum in a parade. His stomach lit up with the fires of anxiety and he started to sweat more than usual. This was a covert mission and attention was the last thing Agent Adrian needed.

When he reached the house, his heart skipped a beat when one of the men addressed him—his cover had been blown.

"Hey," cried a dark, muscular man with flared nostrils and a cruel facial expression, "hold it there, big man. That's too much pizza for a skinny fellow like you."

"I really can't stop," said Adrian, continuing to walk, with a pounding heart.

"Men ain't eat for the day … you got 'bout fifty slices of pizza in that bag … and talking 'bout you can't stop?"

Adrian glanced behind him to see the men rising from the step. In that moment, he was sure his heart would escape its housing, and burst through his chest.

"Get that lil' man!" came a shout from the crowd of men.

Adrian took flight immediately, with the group of men in hot pursuit. He was drained from the walk to Percy's Pizza through the sun, but somehow, he seemed to be propelled by an unknown energy source. He didn't feel the sun anymore, nor did he feel fatigued— he just felt a rush of adrenaline, and knew that the items he had just retrieved could not be allowed to fall into foreign hands.

Adrian dashed through a narrow street, between two blocks of adjoining state-owned apartments. There were eight apartments in each block and a ridge at the end of the street. As Adrian approached the ridge, he could hear the footsteps of the men gaining on him.

"Sha'Tanya said this ridge leads to a very steep descent," he thought, as he saw the ridge getting closer and closer, "if I fall, I'm finished, but if I slow down, I'm finished too."

Adrian maintained his speed as he reached the ridge,

propelling himself through mid-air, over the ridge like a real special agent.

"I can't fall, I can't fall, I can't fall," he thought, as he cleared the ridge and gravity started to pull him down into the descent.

He hit the ground in stride, and managed to retain his balance as he continued his run down the descent with the bag of pizza slices still in hand. The descent was not a smooth run, as the ground was dotted with depressions, partially exposed rocks, patches of slippery grass and loose gravel. As he ran, he heard an expletive, followed by some moans and groans. He glanced behind him to see one of the men's bodies rolling down the incline. The terrain was starting to hurt Adrian's feet through his shoes, and he imagined how it must have felt to the man whose body was now in direct contact with it.

"Look what happened to 'Bad Nasty'," cried one of the men, as Adrian reached the bottom of the descent, "men, we gotta mess-up this lil' man good."

Adrian heard those words, and bolted off with renewed vigour towards a huge wire-fenced playground a short distance away. As he reached the playground, he could hear the men not far behind him.

"They seem to have fresh energy and determination since their friend fell," he thought, as he dashed through the gate and into the playground. "Now I'm fenced in; if Sha'Tanya's info doesn't pan out, I'm as good as mauled."

Adrian bolted through the playground, jumping over a seesaw and dashing through a set of swings, all the while, scanning the fence for a breach.

"What if they patched the fence," Adrian thought, doubting Sha'Tanya's intelligence report as his heart raced, "how would Sha'Tanya even know that there's a hole in this fence—seemed like she avoids this area at all costs."

Adrian's fears were soon alleviated when he saw the breach in the fence—despite abandoning him, Sha'Tanya had proven herself a worthy sidekick. It was not a big breach, but he believed, as Sha'Tanya had stated, that his slender body could get through it with ease. As Adrian reached the breach, he could hear the men behind him, closer than they had ever been. His heart raced as he dropped to the ground and pulled himself through the hole in the fence, as quickly as humanly possible.

As he picked himself up off the ground, on the other side of the fence, the men were struggling to get through the hole already. Adrian knew it was only a matter of time before they made it through, so he wasted no time in dashing for a dirt road between some bushes. The dirt road led to a main road, and Adrian could see a couple of cars passing as he dashed through it.

"The fence bought me some time," he thought, as he reached the end of the dirt road, "I just have to maintain this lead."

Adrian turned left, onto the sidewalk, with the main road to his right and bushes to his left. As he started to run, a sizable crack in the sidewalk caused him to trip and fall flat on his stomach.

"This can't be happening," thought Adrian, as he picked himself up off the sidewalk, "I needed that lead."

By the time he steadied himself, the men dashed around the corner and were upon him. The dark, muscular man who had addressed him earlier from the step, pushed Adrian back down on the sidewalk, back-first, with pizza still in hand.

"I was just going to take away half of the pizza," he shouted, with a cruel look and violent body language, "but now, I want all, and that is after we mess you up for 'Bad Nasty'—your mother ain't gonna recognise you when we get through!"

Adrian closed his eyes tightly, gasping for breath as his face was inundated with saliva, beads of sweat dripping from the man's face and marijuana breath. He could also smell the man's sweat soaked armpits and his lungs didn't seem to be working—he was hyperventilating, in a major panic attack.

Suddenly, the piercing sound of a siren echoed in Adrian's ears, and Adrian heard the men fleeing as the thug's grip was severed. He opened his eyes, now able to see the road again. A police car had passed on the other side of the road and was now turning around to pursue the men. Within seconds, the police car was zooming past Adrian and turning into the dirt road, where the men had apparently fled. The police officers exited the car in the dirt road to pursue the men, but one of the officers ran back to the main road to check on Adrian. By the time he got there, like a true secret agent, Adrian was gone.

THE EVOLUTION OF ADRIAN MANNING

Minutes later, Adrian was back at the school. His shortcut may have been perilous, but it accomplished what he needed it to—he had reached the school with ten minutes to spare. He just had to climb over the wall and get the food to the children. This time, however, he didn't have the luxury of a diversion; he had no way of knowing if the coast was clear, but Agent Adrian had prevailed against incredible odds and he convinced himself that this would be no different.

"The back of the school," he thought, "that's the perfect place of re-entry."

At the back of the school was a secluded, concreted area, with a garbage skip, an emergency water tank and a small building containing the school kiln. It was the perfect point of re-entry; garbage wasn't carried out till the end of school, the water tank was almost never used, and the kiln wasn't operational.

Adrian hooked the handle of the bag he was carrying, around his wrist, and started to climb the tall wall. He pulled himself over the wall and climbed down a bit before jumping down onto the concrete below, between the garbage skip and the water tank. The area was deserted, as usual, and Adrian breathed a sigh of relief as he prepared to make his way to the rendezvous point.

As he started to move, he pondered whether the whole ordeal he had been through was worth it, as he was haunted by Alex's words, "Let's just hope this doesn't turn out like past plans you've had."

He had told Alex that failure perished with the old Adrian, but now, despite the success of his mission, he couldn't help but ponder on that statement. Was he really a new Adrian, or was he still the same old car with a new coat of paint? His actions were driven by a different motivation, but the outcome was the same—turmoil. His past pursuit of popularity had put him in some disastrous situations, but this pursuit of what he considered a noble cause, had put him in the most dangerous situation yet.

Suddenly, Adrian heard a noise from the direction of the building with the kiln. He turned around, heart racing, to see Principal Harding leading two workmen out of the kiln.

"Well, well, well," said the principal, as Adrian froze in his tracks, "this is very disappointing."

Adrian just stood there, frozen, with his heart racing, staring at the principal. Fear had come upon him like a barbell.

"I was so impressed by the maturity I saw in you that I moved to look into your concerns with immediate effect," continued the principal, folding his arms, "I brought in workmen to evaluate the kiln and I even started looking for loopholes in the canteen contract."

Adrian's heart sank as shame and disappointment came upon him like extra weights added to the barbell that was his fear.

"I really thought you had evolved into a new, more mature Adrian," continued the principal, "but now I see clearly who you have become—Suspended Adrian."

CORPORAL CARNAGE

Adrian stood on the ninety-metre-long football field in the early afternoon sun. There were walls to the south and east of the field, stands to the west and school buildings to the north. A driveway, leading to the rear gate of the school, separated the school buildings from the field.

Adrian stood, with eleven other boys, all clad in white t-shirts and red short pants, staring towards a gap in the school buildings; this is where their new physical education teacher would soon appear. There was much speculation about who this new teacher would be, and what he would be like.

"I hear this man is fresh out of the army," said Akanni, a dark Rastafarian with thick lips, "a lance corporal or something."

"That'd better be a rumour," said Jerome, a bony, pale white boy, resembling a whitewashed stick insect, "I'm not cut out for army life."

"Here he comes," cried Adrian, as a thick, clean-shaven, dark man of medium height, with a shiny bald head, walked across the driveway and onto the field. He was wearing an army green shirt and short khaki pants.

"Privates!" shouted the man, with a voice rougher than gravel as he approached the group of boys.

"What kind of class is this," muttered Jerome, "P.E. or biology?"

"Idiot," Adrian retorted, as the man reached the group, "all soldiers begin at the rank of private."

"I am Corporal Cumberbatch," cried the man, firmly and loudly, "and you, Privates, are about to become men."

The boys stared at Corporal Cumberbatch with dumbfounded expressions.

"Yes, sir; thank you, sir," shouted the corporal, suddenly, making Adrian step back a bit, "that is the appropriate response!"

The boys all responded in a synchronized chorus, "Yes sir; thank you, sir!"

"First order of business," yelled the corporal, with his hands behind his back, "two laps around the field."

"Yes, sir; thank you, sir!" shouted the boys, as they started to run.

"Halt," screamed the corporal, "this is not a field; this is an embarrassment!"

The boys looked at each other with discombobulated expressions as the corporal led them off the field and across the driveway into the school. They followed him through the canteen, past the hall, and down a passageway under a long trellis. The passageway led to the office block of the school, and to Adrian's shock, the corporal continued to lead them beyond the office, through the front parking lot and down the worn driveway to exit the school. As the sun's rays illuminated the corporal's shiny head like a lighthouse, their exodus continued, through the school gate, and across the road, to a big pasture.

Adrian had never known who the owner of the pasture was, but he knew it didn't belong to the school. He also knew that it would change the definition of two laps; whereas the school playing field was ninety metres in length, this pasture was one hundred and seventy metres in length. Coupled with a width of one hundred and fifty-nine metres, Adrian was looking at over twenty-seven thousand square metres—and he had to run two laps around it.

"Five minutes starts now!" screamed the corporal, jolting Adrian and the other boys into action.

By the time Adrian had run a third of his first lap, despair had set in; he felt like an ant in the vastness of the field and he struggled to maintain his pace. The sun was also assaulting his body like a jockey whipping a horse with every stride. By the end of the first lap, a gap had formed between Adrian and most of the other sweat soaked boys. This was, however, not as big as the gap that had formed between Adrian and Jerome.

"Run, old men, run!" screamed the corporal as the boys passed him at the end of their first lap.

Adrian looked on in shame, as pedestrians had stopped to watch the spectacle. He resolved to close the gap between himself and the other boys.

"I can't stop him from calling me an old man," he thought to himself as he ran, "but I can at least reclaim some of my dignity by closing this gap; this will not be the whitewashing of Adrian Manning."

Mustering all of his stamina, and all of his willpower, Adrian closed the gap about three hundred metres into his second lap. This triumph had an unintended side effect, however; Jerome was now twice the distance he had been from Adrian on the first lap.

By the time the boys neared the completion of the second lap, Adrian was thoroughly exhausted, and thoroughly soaked. He was pretty sure the other boys were too as they all collectively lost some of their pace.

"People on life support can do better than this," screamed the corporal as Adrian lugged his thin frame across the homestretch, "you are not old men, no, you are old women—pregnant old women!"

By this time, the number of pedestrian spectators had increased, and Adrian could hear them laughing at the corporal's description of the boys as he approached the endpoint.

"Run, ladies, run," screamed the corporal as the boys passed the endpoint, "you are a disgrace to pregnant old women everywhere!"

Finally finished his task, Adrian threw his thin frame on the ground and tried to regain his breath as the onlookers laughed. By the time Adrian had managed to regain most of his breath, Jerome was now finishing his laps.

Corporal Cumberbatch stood, shaking his shiny

head as Jerome crossed the endpoint and collapsed on the ground.

"This expecting senior," started the corporal, pointing at the whitewashed collection of bones that had just collapsed on the ground, "completed the laps thirty seconds too late, and failed to keep up with the troops—that has earned you all another lap."

"But we finished on time, sir," cried Adrian, in despair.

The corporal gave Adrian a stare so cold it sent a shiver down his spine.

"I mean, yes, sir; thank you, sir!" cried Adrian, in fear of retribution.

"The weakest private can be the downfall of the entire unit; you succeed or fail only as a team" replied the corporal, firmly, with his hands behind his back. "You will now do two laps for questioning my instruction—and I will add a lap for every man that falls behind!"

Adrian looked at the other boys as he picked himself up off the ground. Their faces echoed the same feeling he was experiencing—utter bewilderment.

As they started to run, Adrian's bewilderment was sharpened by the corporal's latest remark.

"Shameful, absolutely shameful," cried the corporal, "your fathers must be embarrassed to have you as sons!"

This statement pierced Adrian to the core, more so than any which preceded it. It was in that moment that Adrian made a resolution; the corporal had to be taken out.

By the end of the school day, it was evident that

Adrian wasn't the only person to reach that resolve. That afternoon, as Adrian prepared to exit the front gate of the school, a group of boys came running down the worn driveway shouting his name. Akanni was leading the pack of boys, which consisted of Jerome and the other boys from Adrian's class.

"Something has to be done about Corporal Carnage," cried Akanni, grabbing Adrian by the shoulders.

"I agree—nice name, by the way—but why is everybody staring at me?" replied Adrian with a progression of expressions, going from ponderous, to amused, then to sceptical.

"As much as I hate to admit it," started Akanni, staring Adrian directly in the eyes, "you're a genius when it comes to these things; you took down the biggest bully in the history of this school—Ricardo Thompson."

"This is a teacher!" cried Adrian, staring sternly at Akanni. "Taking him down would require the principal's involvement."

"That's your specialty too," said Akanni, with a smooth voice, "you got Principal Harding to fix the school kiln, and you got him to send Mr. Peters into retirement ..."

"At the end of the year," Adrian interrupted, "we can't go that long with this Corporal Carnage guy."

"I know," said Akanni, with a smile, "we don't just need your sweet-talking mouth, we need your scheming mind to come up with something big."

"My last scheme got me suspended," Adrian replied coldly, folding his arms with a straight face.

"Well, yes—but I'm sure it also made you smarter," said Akanni, forcefully, while making direct eye contact with Adrian, "we're confident that you can take on Carnage and Harding—and win!"

Adrian paused and pondered for a moment. There were definitely reasons not to do it; he wasn't keen to get in trouble again, and Akanni had been an adversary to him more than once in the past. However, there were also reasons to do it; Akanni had been known to work with him in the past for a mutual cause, and most importantly, he fancied himself an intellectual giant and a tactician. To have these boys put so much faith in his tactical intellect was very appealing to him.

"I have an idea," said Adrian, with a gleam in his eyes, as Akanni put his hands in a clasped position and looked on, "but it depends on how badly you want to take down Corporal Carnage."

"Whatever it takes," said Akanni.

"We can't go an entire term like this," came another voice out of the group.

"Whatever you need, I'll pay for it," cried Jerome, with his arms folded. "I'm sure I lost weight today; if I lose any more weight I'll disappear!"

Jerome was filthy rich, and with his support, Adrian knew that his plan could be effective, however, he was still sceptical about whether the boys would buy into it when they actually heard what he had in mind. Nevertheless, he proceeded to share his plan with the group.

"Ok … that's … a little extreme," said Jerome, with a look of great scepticism after hearing Adrian's plan.

"Look, we need to make this a formal protest; we are guaranteed the right to protest peacefully," started Adrian, waving his hands as he defended his scheme with precision. "The protest action has to make a statement strong enough that Principal Harding would want to diffuse it quickly—and the statement should be directly linked to our cause."

There was a hush among the group, as all the boys stood pondering Adrian's breakdown of the plan. It was Akanni who eventually broke the silence.

"I hate to admit it, but Adrian is right and this plan can work," he said, facing the group of boys.

"Desperate times call for desperate measures," said Adrian, with a calm confidence.

"We need some time to think about it, though," said Akanni, turning to look at Adrian.

"Well, we've got a week before facing Corporal Carnage again," said Adrian, to a nod of agreement from the boys.

Adrian walked away from the boys, leaving them to ponder his plan and get back to him.

Throughout the week that followed, different boys from the group approached him with possible alternatives but no one could come up with a more effective plan than Adrian's.

Finally, the day for physical education came around again, and the boys all assembled in the bathroom to change into their P.E. uniforms before the final lunch bell rang. The boys all stood in front of a long changing bench, which faced six toilet stalls on the other side.

"You ready to do this, boys?" asked Adrian, looking

around at everyone in the group.

"We can't come up with a better alternative, so let's get this over with," said Akanni, taking a wig and a red skirt out of his backpack, which was positioned on the bench. "Corporal Carnage was right about one thing; we can only win this as a united team."

The boys all proceeded to put on wigs and red skirts, and pack up their backpacks, concluding their transformation just as the first of two end-of-lunch bells rang.

"After you," said Akanni, allowing Adrian to lead the group out of the off-white bathroom.

Adrian led the way, past the toilet stalls, and through an area with four sinks on their right and a blank wall on their left; this area led to the entrance and exit of the bathroom.

Upon reaching the bathroom door, Adrian's backpack was snatched from him. He turned around quickly to see who had relieved him of his property but before he could assess the situation, Akanni was pushing him through the bathroom door with great force, causing him to stumble backwards through the door and fall to the ground. By the time he picked himself up off the ground, the bathroom door was slamming shut in his face.

It didn't take long for a crowd of children to gather, and it certainly didn't take long for a chorus of laughter to erupt as Adrian, clad in wig and skirt, tried to no avail to force the door open.

He knew he had to think quickly, as the commotion was attracting more students, and would eventually attract the faculty. None of the options available to him were particularly pleasant, but he had to quickly ascertain the path of least humiliation.

Thinking quickly, Adrian snatched the wig off his head, and released the skirt, allowing it to fall to the ground. He then dashed around the building, with his loose shirttail covering most of his undergarment, and made his way to the main office, at the far side of the block.

Some of the children followed him, laughing all the way, while others opted to retrieve and examine his shed garment. Adrian couldn't allow himself to care what the children were doing; he still had to face Corporal Carnage so he had to resolve his situation quickly.

As he mounted the steps to the porch of the office, the final lunch bell rang. He knew that this would disperse the children but it also put him a step closer to being late for physical education.

"Please, I had a mishap," he cried as he ditched the wig and burst through the office door with his heart racing, "I need to borrow a pair of P.E. pants from the sick bay—desperately."

A startled receptionist sprang up from her seat to look over the counter, which was taller than the desktop behind it.

"Of course," said the clear, spectacled woman.

Minutes later, Adrian was running down the worn school driveway, towards the big pasture on which they were to meet for physical education. The feeling of humiliation was still very much with him, but it was now accompanied by raging anger. Corporal Carnage was still his enemy, but Adrian was determined to bring his own carnage to his treacherous classmates, especially the villainous Akanni. He was upset about the humiliation he had just endured, but more upsetting than that, was the fact Akanni and the boys had outsmarted him. That wasn't going to happen again.

"Sorry to be late, Corporal," cried Adrian, as he ran onto the pasture, past the pedestrian spectators, to join the assembly of traitors, all of whom were dressed in their regular uniforms.

"I have an excuse, sir," said Adrian, nervously, as he handed the corporal an official excuse from the office and slotted into the group next to Akanni.

The corporal took the piece of paper and read it with a stern expression, then stared at Adrian intently, sending a sun-defying chill through Adrian's body.

"Private!" shouted the corporal, finally, in his chilling, gravelly voice.

"Yes, sir!" replied Adrian, promptly.

"When you leave your team to be outgunned and overpowered by the enemy," started the corporal with his hands behind his back, "do you think an excuse makes it alright?"

"No, sir," cried Adrian, with a serious face, "it is not acceptable, sir!"

"I'm glad you think so, Private," said the corporal, with a smirk, "because thanks to you, instead of doing ten push-ups, you will all be doing twenty—in perfect sync—starting now!"

"Yes, sir; thank you, sir!" came a chorus, as the boys all dropped to the ground and started their push-ups, in sync with the corporal's counting.

As they were coming up from number three, Adrian glanced at Akanni with a devious grin.

"Four!" shouted the corporal.

Adrian went down with the boys, but didn't come up with them; he purposely lingered longer than he should.

"Halt!" cried the corporal, with hands behind his back. "Private 'Adrianna' can't keep a rhythm—start over!"

The other boys collectively sighed as the corporal restarted the count from number one. This time, Adrian allowed him to get to number ten before breaking the rhythm.

"Halt!" cried the corporal. "Number one, ladies!"

"What do you think you're doing?" Akanni whispered to Adrian.

"Oh, now you want to be on the same page?" whispered Adrian, grimacing from the pain in his arms. "Sorry, can't accommodate you."

Adrian proceeded to break the rhythm again, this time at number fifteen.

"Come on Adrian," cried Akanni, "Jerome is keeping the rhythm; you can't be this bad!"

"Private," shouted the corporal, pointing at Akanni, "I don't remember promoting you—twenty-five push-ups for everyone!"

"Stop it," whispered Akanni to Adrian as they restarted.

"I'll run myself into the ground if it takes you with me," replied Adrian, keeping his resolve despite his arms feeling like they would drop off, "every week of the school year."

"Sorry we turned on you," whispered Akanni, "we'll humiliate ourselves—just please stop."

Adrian stopped sabotaging the push-ups, but by that time, Jerome's frail frame simply could not hold out any longer, and there were three more restarts before the corporal punished everyone with four laps of the field.

Later that afternoon, as Adrian prepared to exit the school through the front gate, Akanni and the other boys came running down the worn driveway shouting his name.

"What do you want?" asked Adrian, coldly, as he turned to face the group.

"It was all Akanni's idea," cried Jerome, "he said he couldn't resist the opportunity to …"

"Shut up!" interrupted Akanni. "That's not important right now—we discussed the matter, we are sorry, and we agree to carry out the plan next week, as we originally planned."

"No, not as originally planned," said Adrian, with a smug smirk, "with one modification."

Adrian then proceeded to lay out his terms for participation in the scheme.

"No, I don't agree to that!" cried Akanni, with passion.

"Then you better start working out," said Adrian, folding his arms, "because I intend to run us all into the ground—every single week."

"No," shouted Jerome, "we'll accept your terms!"

"No, we won't!" Akanni shouted, stamping his foot on the worn pavement.

"Yes, we will," came another voice out of the crowd, as a big, rough looking boy stepped forward and grabbed Akanni by the collar, flanked by all the other boys.

It appeared a decision had been made, voluntarily by most. Adrian turned and walked out of the school with a wide smile of triumph on his face; the tables had turned and he was the one calling the shots now.

The following week, the day for physical education came around again, and the boys all assembled in the bathroom again in front of the changing bench.

"You ready to do this, boys?" asked Adrian, looking around at everyone in the group.

"It seems we don't have a choice," said Akanni, taking a wig and a red skirt out of his backpack, which was positioned on the bench, "but let it be known, I do this under protest."

The boys all proceeded to put on wigs and red skirts, and pack up their backpacks, concluding their transformation just as the first of two end-of-lunch bells rang.

"After you," said Adrian, allowing Akanni to lead the group out of the bathroom.

Akanni gave Adrian a look from hell, then led the way, past the toilet stalls, past the sinks, to the exit of the bathroom.

Upon reaching the bathroom door, Akanni discovered a throng of children waiting to behold the spectacle. Akanni led the boys out of the bathroom to roars of laughter, as Adrian followed—in his regular P.E. uniform—with a deceptively innocent look on his face.

The boys made their way around the block, past the main office, down the worn driveway and across the road to the big pasture, leaving a wake of laughing children behind them. Corporal Carnage had not yet arrived, but the usual pedestrian spectators were gathered, some with umbrellas, others with popcorn. As the boys deposited their bags on the side of the pasture, it was clear to Adrian that the boys' attire was causing a big stir in the crowd; some were openly amused, while others seemed to be somewhat disturbed by it.

Soon, the second lunch bell could be heard in the distance, and Adrian caught a glimpse—through the crowd of spectators—of the corporal's glistening head coming down the driveway.

"He's coming, guys," said Adrian, "it's the moment of truth."

"You'd better live up to your end of the bargain," said Akanni, sternly, with his arms folded.

"Don't worry, Lady Akanni," replied Adrian, with a grin, "I dislike Corporal Carnage more than I dislike you."

Finally, the corporal broke through the spectators with a gravelly shout, "Part!"

Upon penetrating the crowd, he froze, with an astonished look on his face.

"Privates," he bellowed, "what is the meaning of this?"

Adrian looked at the boys and then stepped forward to face the living carnage that stood before him.

"Privates are dutybound to their commanding officers' wishes," started Adrian, with a deceptively firm voice which did not betray his shaking knees, "but we are students, and we are afforded the right to protest when our superiors' actions are detrimental to our development—we will not be emasculated by you or anyone else!"

There was a roar of applause from the spectators, and the corporal looked like he was about to blow a gasket. He turned around as if to address the crowd, just as people were aiming their mobile phones to take pictures.

"All of you," screamed the corporal, turning around again without addressing the spectators, "to the principal's office!"

A few minutes later, they were all in the principal's office, sandwiched between a big trophy cabinet and the principal's huge desk. Behind the desk, sat a tall, clear, slender man, with a ridiculously large Adam's apple and a hairline in greater retreat from his forehead than a defeated army. This was Principal Harding, and he just sat, staring at the boys and the teacher as if trying to decide what to make of the group of boys clad in wigs and skirts.

"Okay," started Mr. Harding, at last, "who wants to go first?"

"I am a corporal," cried Mr. Cumberbatch, quickly and sternly, "and these hooligans have disrespected me by coming to my class in such attire!"

"You boys think this is funny?" asked the principal, staring intently at the group of boys, who were all staring at Adrian. "Is this your idea of a practical joke?"

"There's nothing funny about it, sir," said Adrian, with that deceptive calm he had displayed earlier, "we have been subjected to treatment befitting adult soldiers, and we have been emasculated at every turn."

Adrian tried to read Mr. Harding's face but his cold stare did not betray his thoughts.

"For weeks, we've been called old women, pregnant old women and other emasculating slurs, in the presence of onlookers," Adrian continued, unsure of his persuasiveness but bolstered by the confidence the boys had placed in him, "and these boys are formally exercising their right to protest this injustice, by publicly demonstrating how they have been made to feel inwardly."

Mr. Harding sat forward in his chair, as if his interest had been piqued, but his face did not change. Adrian gave up trying to read him, and just focused on his presentation.

"How are we to be nurtured into the men of tomorrow," Adrian concluded, "when we are systematically denied acknowledgement of our very masculinity?"

The principal paused for a moment, now with a ponderous look on his face. He held his chin as he squinted one eye and wrinkles invaded his forehead, just below the border from whence his hairline had been vanquished. Adrian could feel the tension in the room as everyone awaited his response. Then, finally, he broke his silence.

"I have to decide if you boys have been genuinely damaged," started the principal, "or if this is your idea of a clever stunt."

Adrian took a deep breath before responding. Success or failure could be determined based on his response and he knew he had to come up with something truly compelling.

"Two weeks ago, the corporal told us that our fathers must be ashamed to call us their sons," started Adrian, with a passion he had not displayed up to that point, "those words are still echoing in my head because they could very well be true; I haven't seen my father in ten years, and I don't need my school teachers reminding me of that fact!"

"How was I supposed to know his father was AWOL?" cried the corporal, passionately.

"Enough!" interrupted Principal Harding. "I'm inclined to agree with the boys …"

"You can't be serious," shouted the corporal, "I'm a corporal; they're children!"

"Lance corporal," cried the principal, confirming Mr. Cumberbatch's lower rank while hitting the desk with his hand, "and yes, they're children, not assets on a battlefield, and the fact they've gone to this extreme should tell you that your actions have affected them on a deep level—I will deal with you later!"

Mr. Harding then turned his attention back to the students, as the lance corporal stared at him with fire in his eyes.

"I respect your right to protest—you will get another teacher," started the principal, as the boys openly showed their joy at the decision.

"But I also respect the rules and process," continued the principal, rising from his chair with a tamarind rod in hand, which he seemingly pulled from under the desk, "there are formal procedures for having grievances heard, but you breached the school rules by wearing unsanctioned attire—for that, you will be flogged."

A chill pierced Adrian's body, and it had nothing to do with the air conditioner in the office. As the principal stepped to the side of his desk, Adrian's heartrate shot up like fireworks, until he heard the next words to leave Mr. Harding's mouth.

"Everyone not wearing the correct attire, form a line and come!"

Adrian watched in both relief, and horror, as the boys were flogged one by one with the firm rod, known in student circles as '*The Enemy*'. The reverberation of the blows caused him to grimace and twitch even though he wasn't the one being flogged. This was especially true when Jerome received his allotment of lashes—he had never been flogged in his life and Mr. Harding was unmoved by his vehement protest.

"You can't do this," he cried as he stepped forward, "I'm too rich to be flogged; my maid will take the lashes for me."

Adrian closed his eyes, unable to watch as Jerome was introduced to the rod, and howled like a dog in distress. He feared the rod would fracture Jerome's brittle looking frame.

After Jerome, was Akanni, and Adrian was sure to open his eyes for this flogging. As he stepped up, Adrian looked him straight in the eyes, with a gleam. Akanni gave Adrian a stare so cold Adrian could feel it across the room—until it was melted by the fire of the rod.

Finally, the floggings concluded and the boys were instructed to grab their bags and file out of the office. The boys who had been flogged hurried out of the office before Adrian could even move. Based on their cold glances, Adrian knew that he would have to watch his back for the rest of the term. In that moment, however, he didn't care—it was rare for him to achieve a clean victory and he was intent on savouring the moment. He had been double-crossed and humiliated, but he still solidified himself as an intellectual giant and a master tactician. He managed to get rid of Corporal Carnage, and he also managed to punish his double-crossers with the carnage of corporal punishment. The list of people he had managed to take down was now much longer—Ricardo Thompson, Mr. Peters, Corporal Carnage, Akanni and the entire male population of his class. Adrian felt invincible in that moment—but that moment, like any other, had to end.

As the last of his classmates exited the office, and Adrian prepared himself to follow, Mr. Harding's voice came booming across the room, sending a chill through his body.

"Halt and turn, Mr. Manning!"

Adrian turned around slowly, with a pounding heart, to see the principal sitting back in his chair, staring at him intently.

"It's pretty clear that you are the mastermind behind this frilly stunt," said the principal, with a sly-looking smile.

Adrian just stood frozen, unable to render a response.

"This isn't the first time you've been at the centre of a plot that undermined the rules of this school," Harding continued, his smile changing to a more serious stare. "Your last plot got you suspended, yet, here we are again."

Adrian braced himself for the worst as Lance Corporal Cumberbatch looked on from the side of the room, with folded arms and a grin. His clean victory was slipping away quickly and Adrian pondered his prospects with burning anxiety. Would he be flogged like the others? Would he be suspended again? Which of those was the better prospect? His train of thought was soon derailed as the principal delivered his verdict.

"I've flogged you before and I've given you in-house suspension, yet here we are," started the principal, passionately. "It's clear we need a much more severe punishment!"

Adrian looked Mr. Harding straight in his eyes, and he knew what was coming next. In that moment, the corporal and the office around him disappeared; his entire world went dark with despair as Principal Harding uttered the most dreadful words imaginable.

"I'm going to call in your mother!"

TURNING POINT

Adrian stood on a rocky, unpaved driveway, in the morning sun, and breathed deeply, inhaling the fresh sea breeze. He closed his eyes, and focused on the sounds of waves crashing a short distance away, while enjoying the coolness of the breeze which encompassed his person.

Suddenly, a manmade sound interrupted his intimacy with nature; it was the sound of an engine, coupled with the sound of tyres on gravel. Adrian opened his eyes to see an old, grey sedan approaching. It stopped a metre away from him, and deposited a clear, slim boy of average height. His slender nose had a small hump in the middle of its bridge, like the back of a baby camel. Adrian's face lit up as the boy approached him, carrying two big bags.

"Jay, I'm so happy to see you. Welcome to Turning Point Beach!" he cried. "I don't know how I would have made it through this retreat if you didn't agree to come."

"Wait … wait a minute," said Jay, dropping his bags, "you said this was a fun experience that shouldn't be missed!"

"Well, I may have embellished a bit."

Jay folded his arms and looked at Adrian sternly.

"Look, last month I got suspended for a week and my mother started freaking out," said Adrian, with his hands in a defensive pose, "last week, the principal called her into the office about another incident; she blew a gasket and then signed me up for the church retreat—said she had to move quickly before I became a deviant."

"So, you decided that you should share your torture with someone else?" asked Jay, staring intently at Adrian.

"It's really not that bad; I just thought that having someone I'm close to, would maximise the potential for fun."

"For your sake," said Jay, picking up the bags again, "I had better have fun."

"You will, you will. Now come, let me introduce you to the others."

Adrian led Jay to a group of children and adults a few metres away, next to the first of two beach houses. As he introduced Jay to the counsellors and the children from the church, another vehicle drove up the driveway. The group looked on as a black sedan deposited a large, remarkably dark, flat-faced boy, with a nose like that of a hippo and thick matted shrubbery for hair.

"It can't be," said Adrian, grabbing Jay's arm tightly.

"It is," said Jay.

"No, I have to be dreaming. I had a very lifelike dream recently; this has to be another one."

"Everyone, this is my friend, Ricardo Thompson," said a tall, clear boy in the group, as the newcomer lifted his two bags and brought them towards the group.

"Convinced yet?" Jay asked Adrian, as Ricardo walked up to the group and stopped in front of Adrian and Jay.

Adrian's heart was filled with dread as he made eye contact with Ricardo. He stood frozen, staring at his piercing black pupils, which were encompassed by pronounced veins on a pinkish canvas.

"Adrian," said Ricardo, intently, with a smirk, "so glad I get to spend a weekend with you."

The counsellors soon signalled for everyone to go into the beach houses and setup their rooms. The girls took the peach house to the back of the property and the boys took the green house, which was at the front of the property.

"You were right," Jay said to Adrian as they walked to the house, with a sarcastic tone, "this should be a very fun weekend."

Adrian didn't respond. He was preoccupied with the scenes flashing before his mind's eye. For the first three years of his secondary school life, Ricardo was the biggest bully in the school. Adrian remembered all of his altercations with the bully over the years, as well as other altercations he had witnessed. He especially remembered their last altercation before Ricardo graduated from the school—he had managed to save himself from serious bodily harm by humiliating Ricardo in front of his peers.

He was soon snapped out of his daze as they reached the beach house and Jay pulled him into one of the rooms, quickly claiming it as their bunk.

The beach house was painted mint green on the inside and was mostly wooden, with only the bathroom being constructed with bricks. The side entrance led into the dining room, in the middle of the house, with an eight-seater table. That mid-section also led to three bedrooms, the biggest of which carried two full-size beds, accommodating four children. The second largest bedroom carried a single king-size bed, accommodating three children. Adrian and Jay had taken up residence in the smallest of the three bedrooms, which was furnished with a single full-size bed, flushed against the right wall of the room. Two counsellors made their bunks on sofas in the living room, to the front of the house, which led to a patio. To the rear of the house was a kitchen and a single bathroom.

The children settled in, while the counsellors prepared dinner. After dinner, there was time for one joint session before bedtime for both houses. After the session, Adrian and Jay returned to their room and started preparing for bed.

"I can't believe you brought pyjamas," said Jay, pointing and laughing at Adrian as he unpacked his sleeping attire.

"What do you wear to sleep?" asked Adrian, with a quizzical look.

"Nothing. I sleep in my underwear."

"Not next to me, you don't," replied Adrian, shaking his head.

"Fine!" cried Jay, folding his arms.

That night, Adrian lay in the dark in his pyjamas, next to Jay, in a shirt and shorts, unable to sleep.

"You sleeping yet, Jay?" he asked.

"Not yet," replied Jay, in a groggy voice, from the right side of the bed, next to the wall.

"I hope you are a light sleeper."

"Still worried about Ricardo?"

"Of course! The last encounter we had, he was pretty humiliated; he never recovered his status in the school after that."

"I agree that he's gotta be pretty upset with you," said Jay, turning to face Adrian, "but this is a church event; even bullies have some type of reverence for God and the church."

"I hope you're right," said Adrian, as he closed his eyes, listened to nearby waves breaking and allowed himself to relax.

Several minutes later, he detected a change in light, and opened his eyes to find a small flashlight pointed into his face. He flew up, fearing the worst, and shook Jay, who was sleeping like a corpse.

"This is it," he thought, bracing himself for Ricardo's retribution, as the flashlight was lowered.

As his eyes began to adjust to the light in the room, he realised it wasn't Ricardo at all—it was a girl.

"Be cool," came a voice from the feminine figure.

Adrian recognised the voice from school.

"Sha'Tanya," cried Adrian, "what on earth are you

doing here? You stalking me or something?"

"Error," said Sha'Tanya, "I got an invitation from one of the girls but I couldn't find the place so I not too long got here."

"Okay. Why are you here, in my room?"

"I need to borrow some 'toosepaste'."

"You mean toothpaste?" asked Adrian, performing a facepalm.

Suddenly, Adrian jumped up, realising that his palm connected with a strange substance. Jay was still sleeping like a corpse, but Sha'Tanya was gone and his face was covered with toothpaste.

Adrian violently rattled Jay until the corpse was resurrected.

"This better be good," cried Jay, groggily, as he opened his eyes to see Adrian's face.

"You got pasted," he cried, sobering up and bursting into laughter.

"It's not funny," cried Adrian, "I had another one of those realistic dreams; Sha'Tanya was there, asking for 'toosepaste' and then the next thing I know, I'm waking up pasted."

"Firstly, it is funny. Secondly, why is Sha'Tanya in your dreams; I thought you said you were over this girl."

"I am over her, since third form, but none of that is relevant right now," said Adrian, getting out of the bed and walking to the door, "Ricardo got me and I need to get him back."

"How do you know it was Ricardo?"

"Come on, Jay," said Adrian, turning on the light

from a switch next to the door, "why didn't they paste you too? It would've been easy enough—I was targeted, and I know it was him."

Adrian cleaned his face with a washcloth and retrieved a pouch of toothpaste from his bag, not far from the door, and turned the light off.

"Let's say you are right, and it is Ricardo," started Jay, sitting up in the bed, "why can't you just let it die a natural death?"

"If he had just beat me, that would have been fine," said Adrian, intently, "I concede that he's better than me in that regard, but there's no way I let him outfox me—he's on my turf now."

Adrian exited the room, walking on his toes as lightly and quietly as possible. He stealthily crept to the door of Ricardo's room, just before the living room. Everyone in the room appeared to be sleeping, but Adrian wanted to be sure he was executing a clean operation. He peeped around the corner into the living room and satisfied himself that the two counsellors were fast asleep. He then tiptoed into Ricardo's room, next to the first of two full-size beds. As he raised the pouch of toothpaste and began to uncap it, he heard a voice come out of the darkness, like the voice of an apparition.

"Don't even think about it."

Adrian quickly replaced the cap and ran out of the room on his toes, and back to his room next door.

"Did you get him?" asked Jay, as Adrian took his spot on the bed.

Adrian just grunted.

"That would be a 'no'," said Jay, with a chuckle.

"How did he even know I was there?" started Adrian, "his face was buried in the pillow."

"He's probably a light sleeper with good ears."

"It's okay. I've still got Saturday and Sunday. This was a light, spur-of-the-moment operation. Tomorrow night he'll get a taste of what this brilliant brain can really cook-up."

The following night, bedtime came and Adrian had no plan of action.

"I thought your 'brilliant brain' was going to cook-up a masterful scheme," said Jay, as he laid himself out on the bed.

"I'm still thinking," said Adrian, as he turned off the light and took his place on the bed, "he sleeps on his face … rouses easily … is the first to get out of bed in the morning … I've got a big profile of the target— I'll think of something."

His body relaxed as he listened to the breaking waves in the still of the night, but his mind was far from relaxed.

"I need you to understand something about me, Jay," started Adrian, "for years, I schemed and plotted, trying to be popular …"

"I know this," interrupted Jay, in an exasperated tone, "I've been there to reap the punishment …"

"Let me finish," Adrian cut in, "I wanted to be popular because, well, I guess, I didn't feel valuable."

"I feel like I should say something deep, but …"

"You don't have to say anything, just listen," said Adrian. "I was trying to be someone else, but this year, coming into fourth form, I realised I already had some-thing valuable—my wit and my brains."

"Oh," cried Jay, suddenly sitting up in the bed, "so that's why you can't let this go—if Ricardo outwits you, he's beating you in the one area that makes you feel valuable!"

"Exactly," cried Adrian, "I have to find a way to …"

Suddenly, the quiet of the night was disrupted by screams. Adrian and Jay jumped out of bed and rushed out of the room to see what was happening. By the time they exited the room, all lights were on and the entire house was up, in the central dining room, inves-tigating as well.

"A centipede … running 'bout here," cried Ricar-do, sending everyone into a panic.

A wild hunt for the centipede ensued, but Adrian wasn't looking to hunt.

"This is it," Adrian said to Jay, smiling widely as he gripped him by the arm, "while everyone is in a centipede-induced frenzy, I'll be striking—I need your toothpaste."

"Why do you need my toothpaste," asked Jay, as he dashed back into the bedroom and got his bag, "what's wrong with yours?"

"Mine is white," said Adrian, "yours is a red gel."

"What difference does it make?" asked Jay as he handed Adrian the pouch.

"Ricardo's pillow case is red," said Adrian with a smirk, "and he sleeps face-down."

Jay struggled to contain his laughter as Adrian took

the pouch and slipped into Ricardo's room unnoticed. Several seconds later, Adrian exited the room, returned the pouch to Jay and joined the centipede hunt. Several minutes later, no one had found the centipede and despair began to take over.

"Nobody's sleeping in this house tonight unless that centipede meets death," cried Counsellor Deane, a tall, dark, lanky man with a low haircut.

"This centipede business could derail my entire operation," Adrian thought to himself. "The longer these people are up and about, searching for that creature, the greater the likelihood someone will discover my plot."

Adrian ran into his bedroom and retrieved a small can of insecticide from one of his bags. He then analysed where the majority of persons were searching, and ran into the bathroom—where no one was searching at that point in time. Seconds later, the sound of spraying could be heard coming from the bathroom, and before anyone could investigate, Adrian came bursting through the bathroom door.

"I got him," he cried, "sprayed him and he wriggled out the window and fell to the ground outside. He'll be deceased pretty soon."

The children and counsellors praised Adrian for accomplishing what they had failed to achieve, but Ricardo just stared at him with his arms folded.

With the excitement over, everyone returned to their rooms, turned the lights off and prepared to succumb to unconsciousness. Seconds after Adrian put his head on the pillow, there was a loud cry from Ricardo's room.

"What the bird!"

Adrian smiled from ear to ear as he heard laughter erupt from the room next door. Several seconds later, the light in his room was suddenly turned on and both Adrian and Jay sprang up to see Ricardo standing in the doorway with red toothpaste all over his stern face.

"I know this was you," cried Ricardo, "this ain't over."

Suddenly, Adrian jumped out of the bed with a loud cry and started to franticly pull his clothes off while Jay and Ricardo looked on with shock etched upon their faces. Something had stung or bitten Adrian in his back and he could still feel it moving about in his clothes. As soon as he had pulled the clothes off, a giant centipede dashed out of the heap of clothing on the floor and started moving towards the door. Ricardo grabbed one of Adrian's shoes, which was next to the door, and smote the centipede repeatedly with the force of a wrecking ball. It didn't take long for all the occupants of the house to gather at the bedroom door to see what was going on. Their arrival coincided with an eruption of laughter. As Adrian scratched his back, he looked down to make a startling discovery—he wasn't wearing anything. Adrian jumped into the bed, pulling the sheet over his entire body, as Jay jumped out of the bed with equal haste.

"This ain't happening," cried Jay, "not with me in that bed!"

Under the sheet, Adrian assumed the foetal position, which perfectly represented his state of mind; he felt smaller than he had ever felt before. He wanted the bed to swallow him up and keep him sequestered until the retreat was over. His emotional anguish was underscored by the constant stinging in his back from the centipede venom. From his artificial womb, he could hear Ricardo's voice taunting him.

"I was going to get you back for pasting me, but you got yourself."

He then heard Counsellor Deane's voice breaking up the crowd, ordering everyone back to bed. He then heard the counsellor's calming voice, speaking to him through the sheet.

"I'm going to take your roommate into the dining room. You can get dressed and come to me to get that bite checked out."

Fifteen minutes later, Adrian had exited the womb, antihistamine cream had been applied to the bite and things in the house had returned to normal; the stillness of the night was evident once more, and Adrian was back in bed, next to Jay.

"I can't imagine what you are feeling right now, but I have to ask," started Jay, "is that the same centipede you killed?"

"I needed everyone to go back to bed before someone discovered I had pasted the pillow case," said Adrian, in a low, defeated tone.

"So, wait a minute. Were you planning to tell me the centipede was still loose?"

"Nobody found it; I figured it was gone."

"At least this war between you two is over."

"Over? This is far from over."

"Come on, Adrian. Let it die. He got you … you got him back …"

"Then I got myself … it wasn't a clean victory."

"Who are you really trying to impress," asked Jay, sitting up, "Ricardo or yourself?"

"What are you talking about?"

"You said you started to feel valuable through being smart," started Jay, holding his chin, with a ponderous look, "so if your smart plan doesn't work out, that means you feel worthless, and you're going after Ricardo just to prove to yourself that you have value."

"I invited you because I wanted a friend, not a therapist."

"Fine, then. Speaking as a friend, if you're willing to mess up somebody just so you can feel valuable, you're no different from Ricardo—just another bully."

Adrian never responded to Jay's comment; the conversation died a natural death and Jay slipped into a lifeless sleep. Adrian, however, didn't do much sleeping, as his mind churned, reliving the humiliation for most of the night.

Several hours later, Adrian got out of bed, pulling a small flashlight from under his pillow. He spotted it briefly on Jay, who was sleeping like a mannequin with rigor mortis.

"Maybe Jay's right about me," he thought, "but I can't sleep properly until I redeem myself."

He took the flashlight to his bag and retrieved his toothpaste, as well as lotion and hair grease. Moving stealthily, Adrian slipped out of his room and laid a slippery mixture on the floor, in the doorway to Ricardo's room. With his deed finished, he returned to his room and took his place next to 'the mannequin', where he soon fell asleep.

The next morning, Ricardo rose first, in line with Adrian's profile of him. As he walked through the doorway, he slipped in Adrian's mixture and fell backwards, crashing into the wooden floor about a centimetre from the bed frame. The impact was loud, but it also sent vibrations through the floorboards, waking persons in the surrounding rooms. Adrian's eyes popped open and a smile invaded his face, as Jay remained lifeless, next to him. Adrian's smile was soon vanquished, however, as Ricardo charged into the room seconds later with fire in his eyes.

"I know it was you," cried Ricardo, breathing heavily, "this time you went too far."

Adrian's heart tried to leap out of his chest, as Ricardo charged towards the bed forming a fist. As Ricardo's fist cut through the air towards his face, Adrian narrowly escaped the blow by rolling his body off the bed.

Now on the ground, looking up at the dark hulk towering over him, Adrian realised he was having a rematch he never wanted. His heart went into overdrive as he saw Ricardo's huge foot rise into the air above his body. As the foot suddenly descended with force, hurtling towards his thin frame, Adrian narrowly managed to roll out of the way towards the bed. He completed his roll when he was safely under the bed, but the vibrations from Ricardo's stomp reverberated through the floorboards—and through Adrian's heart.

TURNING POINT

The cover of the bed provided a brief sense of safety for Adrian—very brief. Before Adrian's heart and thoughts could settle, Ricardo grabbed the bed frame and lifted the left side of the bed into the air. Jay's lifeless body rolled over as the bed tilted to the right, until the wall broke his roll. Adrian, now exposed, tried to scamper past Ricardo, who released the bed, allowing its frame to drop with force onto Adrian's back before he could get clear. The lash from the bed frame sent Adrian's body flying into the floorboards, face first, as Jay's body was rolled back into its previous position like a lifeless log.

Ricardo gripped Adrian by the neck, dragged him from under the bed, and threw him, back first, onto the mattress and across Jay's thigh, as he raised his hand in a fist to smite him.

Suddenly, a hand held Ricardo's raised hand by the wrist, and stopped it from coming down—it was Counsellor Deane.

"Break it up," cried Counsellor Deane, as he quickly positioned himself between Ricardo and Adrian, who promptly jumped up off the bed behind him, "there's to be no fighting at this retreat!"

Adrian stood, just in front of the bed, staring past Counsellor Deane into Ricardo's pinkish fiery eyes as he huffed heavily.

"I played nice but he carried things too far!" cried Ricardo. "I nearly burst my head and I could've hurt my back!"

"Ok, this is serious, and Counsellor Warton and I take it very seriously. Can we please agree to go out on the patio and deal with this maturely?"

Ricardo reluctantly agreed and Counsellor Deane ordered the crowd that had gathered behind them to disperse as he led the boys through the living room and into the patio—Jay was still as motionless as a statue with paralysis.

Out on the cool, breezy patio, Counsellor Deane sat in the middle of the two boys, all on beach chairs.

"I'm sorry," started Adrian, with a bewildered look, before the counsellor could speak, "I was so mad to get Ricardo, I didn't think about how dangerous my prank could be."

"Why are you so mad to get Ricardo?" asked Counsellor Deane.

"He started it!" cried Adrian.

"Because you made my last year in school a living hell!" cried Ricardo, pounding the arm of the chair.

"Because you've been a bully to me for three years," cried Adrian, reliving all the times Ricardo had made him feel small, "everyone was happy when you got humbled, because all you ever did was make us feel small and worthless."

"Okay. Clearly this issue between you is deep-rooted," said the counsellor. "Ricardo, why do you think you've been a bully all these years?"

"Big man, I ain't had anything else," cried Ricardo, passionately, "bullying is all I had going for me—real talk!"

"Surely you don't believe that's the extent of your value," said the counsellor, looking Ricardo in the eyes.

"You really wanna do this?" cried Ricardo with his arms folded.

"Please," said the counsellor, in a soft voice, as Adrian silently looked on, "your feelings are important and I sense that there are some important things you need to say."

"Look, I ain't smart like Adrian; I had to cheat to pass most of my promotion exams," started Ricardo, in a frank manner. "I ain't handsome like other people; my whole life, people told me that I look like tar."

"Children can be thoughtless and cruel but you can't allow them to …"

"Big man, I ain't just talking 'bout children; when my father left, he told my mother I was too black to be his child," Ricardo interrupted, causing Adrian to stare at him intently. "Too black … too ugly … the only thing that ever made me special was my size, so I had to be a bully!" cried Ricardo, before jumping up from his seat and dashing out of the patio.

Counsellor Deane rushed out of the patio behind him, followed closely by Adrian, as he barrelled down the driveway towards the beach.

"Come back, Ricardo, the beach is off-limits!" cried Counsellor Deane, as Ricardo crossed the road at the end of the driveway and ran onto the beach. "Turning Point is a very dangerous beach!"

Ricardo ran onto the sand, several metres from the breaking waves, and turned around to face his pursuers with hands outstretched, gesturing them to stop.

"I just want to be alone right now," he said, "I ain't saying anything else."

Counsellor Deane stopped, with Adrian behind him, as Ricardo turned around to face the incoming waves.

"Let me talk to him," Adrian whispered to the counsellor.

"You sure that's a good idea?" he asked.

"We'll find out."

As Adrian started his walk towards Ricardo, the fresh, salt air that rushed his nostrils was juxtaposed by the rush of emotion he felt. He'd looked at Ricardo many times in the past, but this was the first time he saw more than just a bully—this was the first time he saw a person, one with some of the same vulnerabilities as himself.

"Last night, Jay said I was no different from Ricardo," he thought to himself as he approached Ricardo's position, "maybe he's on to something."

"You gotta love pain," said Ricardo, as Adrian stood next to him, looking out over the tall breaking waves.

"I think I get it; my father left too," started Adrian, "and it hurts up to this day because I figured he would want to be a part of his son's life, but clearly, I wasn't valuable enough for him to stay."

Ricardo turned and looked at Adrian with his arms folded, making Adrian feel very uneasy.

"Was this the latest in my series of mistakes?" he asked himself, as pain throbbed in his back from the lash of the bedframe and his heartrate started to increase.

"You got my attention," said Ricardo, to Adrian's relief, "I'm listening."

"Listening to you just now on the patio," started Adrian as his heartrate returned to normal, "it felt like somebody turned me inside out."

"Interesting," said Ricardo, turning to face Adrian.

"From trying to be popular, to taking up people's causes, all my plots and schemes, I was just trying to feel valuable," Adrian continued. "You said your size was the only thing that made you feel special; well, right now, being smart is the only thing that makes me feel special."

"I guess that makes sense," Ricardo replied, looking as though he was deep in thought.

"So, I felt like I would have nothing going for me at all if you were to outsmart me."

"Exactly!" cried Ricardo, throwing his hands in the air. "I couldn't let you hurt me and get away with it; being tough is all I have."

"I'm really sorry about this weekend … and your last year at the school."

"Yeah, sorry 'bout the last three years."

Ricardo extended his hand and the boys shook hands for the first time ever.

A short while after, the boys returned to the house with Counsellor Deane. Adrian was upbeat after his unexpected truce with Ricardo. As he returned to his room to prepare for a shower, Jay was stretching and yawning, as if now awaking.

"What happened last night," asked Jay, "did you get Ricardo?"

Adrian facepalmed himself, and proceeded to prep for a shower.

The rest of the retreat was fun and without incident. The counsellors confiscated and managed all toothpaste and creams as a precautionary measure, but all of the boys gelled well, including Adrian and Ricardo. The counsellors tailored many of the remaining sessions to deal with the topic of self-worth, as a result of Adrian and Ricardo's altercation.

The last day of the retreat was a Monday; it was a public holiday, and the children were scheduled to leave late in the morning. As Adrian packed his bags, he recounted the events of the previous morning. For the first time in his life, he had clarity on how he truly felt about himself—deep down inside, he didn't feel valuable. He had proven that this couldn't be fixed with popularity nor intellect, and he knew that this would be a turning point in his life—a major step in the evolution of Adrian Manning. He never suspected such a positive turning point could come about because of Ricardo.

A little later that morning, as everyone stood in the driveway with their bags, awaiting their respective rides home, Adrian stood next to his former nemesis, Ricardo, who was eating a large pack of cream filled sandwich cookies.

"Guys, I had a good time this weekend, and made some unexpected friends," said Ricardo, putting his arm around Adrian's shoulder, "I know it's not much but I have to share these cookies with you guys."

Ricardo pointed the pack at each of the boys present, allowing them to take a cookie, ending with Adrian.

"No hard feelings," he said to Adrian, as he held the pack towards him.

Adrian smiled as he took a cookie from the bag. He was happy that despite the dread he had felt at the beginning, this adventure was actually ending on a positive note.

He put the cookie in his mouth and started to chew it, stopping shortly after—the vanilla cream filling in his cookie was replaced with toothpaste.

"As I said," started Ricardo, smiling as Adrian stared intently at him, "no hard feelings, but I did owe you one."

Adrian at LIBERTY

After years of ill-fated schemes, Adrian has finally reached a turning point in his life.

Now, he's a pretty well-adjusted sixteen-year-old, preparing to graduate secondary school with academic distinction.

The schemes might be gone, but even with the purest of intentions, the adventure and peril that underscored his formative years still occasionally pop up.

As present and past situations collide, startling revelations occur, eventually causing him to consider one last scheme; a scheme with the highest stakes and possibly the greatest danger he has ever faced—but also the greatest reward!

Danger, suspense, humiliation, mistrust and selfless sacrifice all come together, making Adrian's last year of school a year to remember.

Will the life-altering perils ahead all be worth it in the end? Find out in this engaging but poignant conclusion if the perils might just lead to the ultimate thing to put Adrian at liberty.

Redcore
PUBLISHING